Nate dove, stretched all the way out, and caught the ball with the tips of his fingers. But as he came down, the ball jarred loose in front of the goal. It was rolling free, and Nate was still on the ground.

Oshima had charged the goal for a follow-up, and he was about to bang the ball home when Nate reacted. He scrambled up and got a foot under him, and then he dove at the ball as it rolled away from him.

He got his hands on the ball just as Oshima kicked...

*Books about the kids from Angel Park:*

## Angel Park All-Stars

## Angel Park Soccer Stars

# ANGEL PARK SOCCER STARS

## 2

# DEFENSE!

# By Dean Hughes

### Illustrated by Dennis Lyall

Bullseye Books • Alfred A. Knopf
*New York*

Library of Congress Cataloging-in-Publication Data
Hughes, Dean, 1943–
Defense! / by Dean Hughes ; illustrated by Dennis Lyall.
p.    cm. — (Angel Park Soccer stars ; 2)
Summary: Nate Matheson, goalie for the Angel Park soccer team, tries
to find a way to motivate the team's defensive players.
ISBN 0-679-81543-0 (pbk.) — ISBN 0-679-91543-5 (lib. bdg.)
[1. Soccer—Fiction.]   I. Lyall, Dennis, ill.   II. Title.
III. Series: Hughes, Dean, 1943– Angel Park Soccer stars ; 2
PZ7.H87312De   1991   [Fic]—dc20   91-8281
RL: 4.6
First Bullseye Books edition: October 1991

Manufactured in the United States of America
10  9  8  7  6  5  4  3  2

*for Christopher Archibald*

# ★1★

# Tough Match

The San Lorenzo Kickers had kept the pressure on attack, even though they hadn't scored. Nate Matheson, the goalie for the Angel Park Pride, had already made at least a dozen stops.

Two of the Kickers' forwards, the red-headed Vandegraff brothers, were from Holland, where they had learned great soccer. They were a year apart in age, but they were both spectacular players. There were faster players in the league, but no one had better dribbling or shooting skills.

All the same, the Pride was battling, and

with less than twenty minutes left in the first half, the score was still 0 to 0 in this first match of the preseason tournament.

And here were the Kickers, coming hard again.

Nate got ready.

He saw Peter Vandegraff break into the clear and take a pass from the wing. Peter faked a move to the right, and Sterling Malone, an Angel Park fullback, took the fake.

That's all the room Peter needed.

He broke to the left and then *fired* a shot on goal.

Nate was in a good position, though. He dove to his left and stretched out in the air. The ball was coming fast, but Nate slammed it with his fist and knocked it away from the goalpost.

The Kickers' wing controlled the ball and then lifted a crossing pass in front of the goal.

This time Klaus Vandegraff broke to the middle and tried to head the ball. But Nate leaped and snatched the ball out of the air before Klaus could get his head on it.

Quickly, Nate darted into the clear and punted the ball as far as he could. He had stopped another goal, but the Kickers weren't letting up.

"Come on, Brian," Nate screamed at his sweeper. "I need more help. You've gotta back up the other fullbacks!"

Brian Rohatinsky was running upfield. If he heard Nate, he didn't show it.

And Nate was mad. "They all want to score," he mumbled to himself. "No one wants to play defense."

But he had little time to complain. The Kickers were already on attack again, and the Angel Park Pride was falling back on defense.

The left wing was *fast*. And he was breaking down the touchline.

Normally, a fullback would be marking him. But for some reason, all the fullbacks were upfield. So Henry White, the Pride's right wing, moved in tight on the Kickers' wing. Henry was running with him step for step.

He even got a foot in and knocked the ball away. But it rolled across the touchline, and the Kickers got the throw-in. A midfielder tossed the ball long to Peter, who was cutting toward the goal, but Brian got up in the air and headed it back upfield.

The midfielder, breaking into the middle after his throw-in, leaped for a header of his own. He popped the ball toward the side of the field and back to the quick right wing.

The race was on again, and Henry had to cover. He stayed in a good position to keep the wing wide and to cut off his angle for a crossing pass.

"Good job, Henry!" Nate yelled as the wing broke off his run and looked for help from his teammates.

Henry moved in for a tackle, and the two battled until the ball flipped away and a Kickers' midfielder trapped it. Clayton Lindsay, the Pride's star midfielder, marked the man quickly.

"Good work. Fall back, Brian," Nate yelled,

and for once he felt the team had gotten back and set up well on defense.

The Kickers backed off a little, took the ball away from the goal, and set up for another attack. They made a few passes back and forth, but they were well marked.

And then Peter Vandegraff made a break across the field in front of the goal area. The left wing lifted a center pass toward him.

"Jared, *cover!*" Nate yelled, but Jared Trajillo was slow getting to Peter. By then Klaus had caught up with the ball and had controlled it by reaching high with the inside of his foot.

Without hesitating, he slammed the ball to Peter, who was a full step in front of Jared.

At the same time, Patty Pinelli, the left wing and one of the Kickers' best shooters, also sprinted toward the goal.

And the defense broke down.

Tammy Hill and Sterling both covered Klaus, and Pinelli was all by herself.

Peter was moving fast across the goal and

might have had a shot, but Patty had a better one. Sterling tried to leave Klaus and get to her—but too late. She took a pass from Peter, controlled the ball, then charged straight at Nate.

Nate broke toward her to cut off her shooting angle, but she saw that and *blasted* the ball to the left. Nate dove, but he missed the ball by inches, and it caught the corner of the net.

*"Finally!"* Pinelli yelled, and she pumped her arm.

And then her whole team surrounded her. "It's about time!" one of them said. "We should have had a *bunch* of goals by now. These guys aren't any good."

"We should have had about five goals by now!" someone else yelled. "This is the worst team we've ever played."

Nate picked up the ball and tossed it to the referee. The Kickers bothered him, but he was twice as angry with his own players.

"Sterling! Tammy!" he yelled. "What were you thinking about? You don't even *care* about playing defense."

"Lay off, Nate!" Tammy said. "We just messed up."

Sterling wasn't a guy who lost his temper very often. But he spun around and yelled, "Yeah. Shut up, Nate! These guys are good. *You* come out and try to stay with them!"

Nate didn't answer. He knew Sterling was right—in a way. He was sorry he had said anything.

But he also knew that Sterling loved to get upfield. He had been a star on the Angel Park baseball team, and he was used to hitting and scoring runs. But on the soccer team, Coach Toscano had asked him to use his speed to help out on defense.

And who wanted to play defense? Everybody wanted to play forward.

Nate could see the whole field from his position in the goal. He knew what it took to win soccer games. The great teams all played tough defense.

Nate glanced at Coach Toscano. He wished the coach would give the defense a good chewing out. But the coach never did that.

Nate also scanned the fans in the bleachers. His dad had promised to come to the game—if he could make it. But Nate didn't really expect him. His parents almost never came.

The Angel Park players walked upfield for the kickoff. But Heidi Wells, a forward for the Pride, yelled, "Good job, Nate. You're keeping us close. We'll get that goal back."

Jacob Scott was still standing by Nate. He was a rookie at competition-level soccer, but the coach was trying him at a forward spot. He and Nate and Heidi had been working out together almost every day.

Jacob needed the help. The teams in the desert country of Southern California played first-rate soccer even in the under-twelve league. A lot of kids played year round. But Jacob had always given most of his attention to baseball.

"I don't know how we're going to score," Jacob said to Nate. "We're not getting the ball into shooting position."

"I know," Nate said, but he didn't have

time to say all he was thinking. The coach always said that it was defense that created attack opportunities—and *goals*.

For now, however, Nate had other things to worry about. The Pride put the ball in play, but the Kickers were soon on attack again. They had moved the pace up a notch, too. Nate could see that they were feeling confident now that they had taken the lead.

Clayton seemed just as determined to stop the Kickers. He did a great job marking his man in the middle. He stayed with him step for step, whether the guy had the ball or not.

Lian Jie, the other Angel Park midfielder, worked hard too. But Trenton Daynes, who had just come into the game as a substitute fullback, let Peter get behind him.

Peter took a pass from his midfielder and came toward the goal area, unmarked. Tammy moved quickly to cover him. That left Klaus open.

"Brian, cover in the middle!" Nate yelled,

and Brian ran in that direction. But the Kickers had seen the mistake, and Peter kicked the ball to Klaus.

Trenton was falling back fast, and Clayton and Lian were moving in to help.

The Kickers acted quickly while they had the advantage. Klaus fired a shot before Brian could get to him. Sterling saw the ball coming and tried to break toward the goal to help Nate.

He was a split second too late, and the ball slipped past him. Luckily, however, Klaus had not really hit it well.

Nate was able to jump up for the ball, catch it on his fingertips, and come down with it.

He pulled the ball in to his middle and held tight as he hit the ground. And then he ran forward and kicked it to the left side.

The Pride broke upfield to go on attack.

And all the fullbacks blasted ahead at the same time. No one stayed back.

Chris Baca, the Pride's left wing, took the ball and started upfield, dribbling.

Chris was quick, but a Kicker fullback made a good tackle and popped the ball loose. The Kickers' wing picked it up.

Suddenly, the Pride had to switch back to defense. But Brian and Trenton didn't see the tackle for a moment and didn't reverse themselves quickly enough.

The Kickers' right wing passed to Peter, who was breaking down the middle with no one on him.

He drove the ball forward until Sterling picked him up. Then he dropped the ball back to Klaus, and *bam!*—Klaus cut past Sterling and blasted an instep shot. The ball flew past Nate so fast that he had no time to react.

*Goal!*

Just like that, the score was 2 to 0.

Nate stood with his hands on his hips. He shook his head. "We gotta play defense," he said. "We *all* have to play defense."

But no one was listening.

# ★ 2 ★

## Kicked

After the second goal, the Kickers seemed to let up on the pressure just a little. The Pride finally started getting the ball into scoring position.

But the Kickers' fullbacks were rugged, and the Angel Park players never got off a decent shot.

Then some good luck helped out the Pride.

Jacob received a good pass, but the defenders doubled him. He was almost frantic trying to find somewhere to pass the ball.

The defenders had him trapped. And

then they messed up. When one of them knocked the ball away, both defenders blasted out to chase it down. They got their legs tangled and knocked each other to the ground.

Jacob charged ahead, controlled the ball, and dribbled toward the goal. The defense was packed, and the two defenders were quickly up and after him.

When he saw he was about to be marked again, he took a long shot that had little chance of getting through. But the ball bounced off the Kickers' sweeper and rebounded in front of Heidi near the right side of the goal.

She beat her defender to the ball and *slammed* it home. The Pride had scored!

The confidence of the Angel Park players suddenly soared.

"Hey, we can still beat these guys!" Billy Bacon was yelling from the sidelines. "They aren't as good as they think they are."

But the Pride players seemed to think only of scoring and tying up the game.

Just before the half, Clayton dribbled down the middle and lost the ball. The Angel Park fullbacks were pushing on the attack, and a Kickers' midfielder picked off the ball and broke away, ahead of everyone.

Nate was left with no help at all. His only hope was to charge the midfielder and try to cut him off.

He got himself in good position and tried to dive on the ball just as the midfielder entered the goal area, but the ball bounced off Nate's hands, and the midfielder chased it down.

Nate scrambled up, but the goal was wide open.

The midfielder punched the ball into the net, and the Kickers had their two-goal lead back.

Just like that.

Nate was furious. "You guys can't get beat like that!" he screamed at his fullbacks. "What have I been telling you?"

When halftime came, Nate sat down with

the others. He expected the coach to yell at the team, and he wanted to hear it.

But Coach Toscano said, "Fullbacks, I'm glad you want to be part of the attack, but your primary responsibility always has to be defense. You can't all get drawn up too far."

That was it.

And he didn't even sound angry.

"Coach, they're not even *trying* to play defense," Nate said. The anger in his voice was clear.

"Shut up, Nate," someone in the back mumbled, and suddenly Nate really lost it.

He spun around. "You all want to be heroes and score goals!" he yelled. "You leave me back there to cover the goal by myself. That's stupid. You can't play soccer that way!"

"Wait a minute," the coach said.

But Nate was still going. "It makes me sick to see the game played all wrong. All the books say that you have to—"

"Nate, that's enough!" the coach said.

And Nate knew that he had to shut up. But he heard someone imitate him in a high-pitched voice, "All the books say—"

And then he recognized Brian's voice. "Nate knows *everything* about soccer. Aren't we lucky?"

"I know a lot more than you!" Nate barked back at him.

"Team, that's it!" Coach Toscano said. "I won't listen to any more of this!" He had never sounded angry before, but he sounded that way now.

Suddenly, everyone was silent.

"Now, listen to me. Nate is right. Great teams are built around a solid defense. But there is one thing more important. Great teams play together. They support each other."

Nate looked down at the grass. He knew that was also true.

Even when he had been yelling, he knew that it was the wrong thing to do. But he was so frustrated.

And then Coach Toscano began to laugh. "Come on, kids, let's not be so serious. We're here to have fun. And to learn."

Nate just couldn't believe it.

Didn't the guy even *care?*

Coach Toscano did give the players some good instructions on falling back into defensive positions, but he didn't make it sound like that big of a deal.

Nate just didn't understand. If the coach didn't really pound on these guys, would they ever get it through their heads what they had to do?

Coach Toscano knew his soccer, but maybe he would never get the Pride to play the game right.

And so, as the second half began, Nate was still worried.

And things soon got worse.

The Angel Park fullbacks tried to do a better job on defense. But when the team got a good drive going and got the ball well up into the Kickers' territory, all the attention seemed to switch to the attack.

That wouldn't be so bad, except that the players didn't react quickly enough when the ball changed possession.

The Kickers knew how to play intense defense and then steal a pass and immediately go on attack.

Too often, that extra second or two put the Pride defense on its heels, and the Kickers moved up and got off a shot before the defense could get itself set.

Nate knew he had never played better. He gave up one more goal, but he stopped half a dozen good shots.

He also tried to keep his temper under control.

He yelled instructions to his defenders, trying to guide them to help each other. But he didn't want to get mad again.

And then something happened that he just couldn't handle.

Clayton made a great move to intercept a pass and break up the field ahead of his defender. Lian was with him, and Clayton passed off to him. Lian kicked the ball quickly over to Chris, and then took a pass back.

It was all perfect, and Nate cheered for them as they moved up the field away from him.

As the Pride moved toward the Kickers' goal area, Jacob took a pass and moved in for a shot. Once again, though, two defenders covered him.

Clayton was in a good position for a pass, but Jacob was struggling to keep control of the ball.

Sterling broke toward him to help, and that pulled him in very close to the goal area.

Just as Sterling broke toward Jacob, one of the fullbacks kicked the ball loose, and the other one saw Sterling's man break upfield. The fullback lofted a long pass upfield, and Klaus Vandegraff chased it down—ahead of everyone.

He broke toward the goal with his wing, Patty Pinelli, not far behind him.

The Angel Park fullbacks got back as fast

as they could. But Klaus was faster. Sterling was the one who could have stayed with him, but he had been caught way out of position, and no one had dropped back to cover for him.

Klaus raced toward the goal area, dribbling the ball. Brian, running without the ball, was able to catch him, but just as he did, Klaus dropped the ball to Pinelli.

She took the ball straight at Nate until he had to charge her to have any chance. But as soon as Nate came out, she chipped the ball high to Klaus.

Klaus beat Brian into the air and slammed the ball with his head. Nate couldn't get back to the goal, of course, and the net was open. *BAM!* The score was 5 to 1.

Nate hadn't had a chance.

He was steaming mad.

Sterling had made a mad run down the field and, with his good speed, had come close to getting in on the play. But that only left him standing there, looking straight at Nate when the play was over.

"*Sterling!*" Nate yelled. "What were you thinking about?"

"I was thinking about scoring a goal. That's what. Sometimes you have to take a chance, Nate."

"Only if someone else stays back. You guys all got sucked in. You're playing like *idiots.*"

Sterling jumped at Nate and grabbed his shirt. Just then, Jacob came running up and jumped in between them.

"Come on, you guys," Jacob said. "Don't do this."

But Nate didn't have to be told.

He already knew he had blown it again. And he felt rotten. Why couldn't he keep control of his big mouth?

But just then Billy came running to Nate. "Give me your goalie shirt," he said. "The coach sent me in for you."

"*You?* You're going to play goalie?"

It was nuts. The guy was short and slow. He wouldn't have a chance.

Nate looked at the coach. Had he gone crazy?

But Coach Toscano was waving for Nate to come to the sideline.

Nate pulled his shirt off. But he didn't hand it to Billy.

He tossed it on the ground.

# 3

# Chewed Up and Spit Out

Billy was a disaster as a goalie.

The final score was 8 to 1, and it would have been worse if the Kickers hadn't lost interest once the game was out of reach.

Nate stood on the side and suffered. He knew the Kickers were a better team than the Pride. But not *that* much better.

All summer he had worked out on his own, or with Heidi, waiting for soccer season. He had just *known* that the team would be good this year.

And the last couple of weeks the players had started to show that he was right.

And now *this*.

But the worse part was that Coach Toscano still didn't seem to care. He yelled instructions, but he didn't get upset with all the mistakes.

Nate had really thought the Pride had a chance to win the tournament. But the coach had given up all hope when he put Billy in the goal. Nate just couldn't understand that.

After the game Coach Toscano talked to the team about playing better defense, and he told them to show up an hour before the game the next day. He wanted to work out some of the problems they had been having.

But then he said, "Kids, we made some mistakes, and this match got out of hand. But we're not that bad."

Then he laughed. "Hey, come on. Get your heads up. We go into the loser's bracket of the tournament now, but we can still take the consolation championship."

"That's right," Billy said. "Let's *kick* somebody tomorrow and show 'em we're not that bad."

Billy was probably the last guy to be talking big, but then, that was Billy.

Still, the coach didn't mind. "That's right," he said. "We're going to learn from this match. And tomorrow we'll be better than ever. Right?"

The kids all shouted, *"Right!"*

That was all fine and good, but Nate wanted to see something more than yelling in the next match. He wanted to see some serious defense.

The coach told the kids to get some rest and be ready to go the next day. Then, as the players started to walk away, he said, "Nate. Sterling. I want to talk to you."

The two boys stepped up to him, but the coach waited until the others walked away before he spoke.

"Boys," he said in a calm voice, "I'll put up with mistakes. I'll put up with kids who don't play this game very well."

He looked right into Nate's eyes.

"But . . . I will *not* put up with two of my players yelling at each other. Not in practice, and not in a game. If it happens again, you are both *off the team*. Do you understand what I'm saying?"

Nate was taken by surprise. Coach Toscano was suddenly *all* business. His eyes were still locked on Nate.

The two boys nodded.

"Soccer is a game of eleven people who have to be *one team*. It cannot be played by people who won't work together."

Nate took a deep breath. He knew that the coach was right. "Coach, it was my fault, not Sterling's," Nate said.

"Yes, I would agree, for the most part," the coach said. "But Sterling could have walked away and let you cool off—and let *me* deal with you. He didn't have to grab you like that. You looked like enemies out there."

Sterling looked down at the grass. "I'm sorry," he said.

"All right." The coach put a hand on a shoulder of each of the boys. "We'll have no more of it. Shake hands with each other."

Nate reached out quickly and said, "I'm sorry, Sterling."

"Sorry, Nate," Sterling answered.

"One more thing," the coach added. "Nate, you're right about the mistakes the team is making. And you're the one who has to direct the defense. But directing is not blaming people and accusing them."

"I don't know what to do, Coach. I keep telling them that they have to—"

"You have to *lead* them, Nate."

Nate stared at the coach for a moment. He tried to think what that meant. "How do I do that?"

Suddenly Coach Toscano laughed. "Ah, now that's the hard question. But I want you to find the answer. I can do some things, but a team needs a leader on the field. And when it comes to defense, that has to be the goalie."

Nate promised to try his best. Then he

walked over to his friends Heidi and Jacob, who were waiting for him.

"What's the matter?" Heidi said. "What did the coach tell you?"

Nate shook his head slowly, and then he said, "I've got to stop yelling at people—and try to *lead* them."

Heidi nodded as though she knew what he meant. But Jacob was still new to soccer. "How are you supposed to do that?"

"The goalie has to call out to everyone to make sure they cover the right people and stuff like that."

"I know," Jacob said. "But what if they mess up? Aren't you supposed to tell them?"

"I don't know for sure," Nate answered. "I can't do it the way I've been doing it. That just makes everyone mad."

Jacob's parents were walking over now. So were Heidi's, but Nate's had never shown up.

Mr. Wells put his arm around Heidi's shoulder. "I think it's better just to forget that one," he said. He had the same square-cornered smile that his daughter had.

"Forget what?" Heidi said. "Was there a match here? I know *we* didn't play soccer today." She sounded disgusted.

"Hey, come on," Mr. Scott said. "It was only a game. Let's all go cry into a bowl of frozen yogurt."

"No, thanks," Nate said. "I've got to get home."

That wasn't exactly true. But he was in no mood to laugh and eat yogurt. He had a lot on his mind. He had to figure out how he was supposed to *lead* his players.

"We'll walk home with Nate," Heidi said.

And so the parents left, and the three friends walked home together.

As they left the park, Jacob asked Nate, "So what are you going to do? What do you think the coach was talking about?"

"I don't know," Nate said.

But Nate didn't want to tell his friends what he was really thinking. He knew a lot about soccer, and he felt that he was a good player. But he didn't believe that he was a leader.

"Your dad's a big boss at the place where he works," Heidi said. "Why don't you ask him how he gets people to do what he wants them to do?"

Nate laughed a little. "My dad doesn't care about soccer," he said. "If I asked him he'd say, 'Nate, don't take it so seriously. Just go out there and have a good time. After all, it's just a game.' "

"Well, he's right in a way, Nate," Heidi said. "Sometimes you do take it too seriously."

Nate didn't know how to explain how he felt about that. He loved soccer. His dream was to be on a team that played the game the way it *could* be played. He didn't know how *not* to take soccer seriously.

When Nate didn't say anything, Jacob said, "I know how you feel, Nate. When players act like they don't care, I get mad too."

That was fine. But it still didn't answer

the question. How was he supposed to lead his team? Everyone was already mad at him. Anything he did now would probably only make things worse.

"I've got an idea," Heidi said. "You could train everybody like you do animals. Every time they do something right, you could give them a lump of sugar or a dog biscuit—or something like that."

Nate shook his head and said, "Yeah, right." He didn't feel like laughing.

"No, I'm serious. It's just like in school. Look how teachers put smiley faces on your papers and math and stuff. They learn that in college. My mom told me about it. I think they have to take a whole class where they're taught exactly when and where to put the smiley faces. It's all very scientific."

"What are you talking about?" Jacob said.

Heidi was smiling now. "It's true. They tell teachers not to make kids feel bad all the time. They're supposed to watch for positive stuff and then plaster it with stars, or give you a hug or something."

"They better not hug me," Jacob said.

But Nate was really thinking about it. Maybe he did need to compliment the players more. He could try to tell them when they did something right. That was probably the best way.

And yet, he had done that a lot already.

It was the mistakes that he couldn't seem to let pass by.

"Here's what you do," Heidi said. "Every time a player does something good, run out and give him a big hug and a kiss. I happen to know that Tammy would not mind *at all* if you did that a few times in every match. Or even at practice."

"I don't know," Jacob said. "If he kisses Billy, Billy might punch him out."

"Well, okay. Maybe he could just shake Billy's hand and say, 'Very nice job, young man. I'm very proud of you.' Something like that."

Nate shook his head again. He tried not to smile, but he did anyway.

Heidi wasn't finished. "Maybe he could

put a star on Billy's forehead—or draw a smiley face on him."

"Uh . . . I don't think so. A coupon for a cheeseburger would probably be the best bet with Billy."

"Now you're talking," Heidi said, and she burst out laughing.

Nate finally laughed too.

But he was still worried.

# ★ 4 ★

# Another Day, Another Game

The next game of the tournament was against the Cactus Hills Racers. Jacob told Nate that he knew some of the players. They had been on the Cactus Hills baseball team—the Reds.

"Jimmy Gerstein is the one with the big mouth," Jacob told Nate.

"Hey, you don't have to tell me about him," Nate said. "He played soccer last year. He thinks he's the greatest player of all time."

About then Gerstein yelled, "Hey, Scott, you guys must not have much of a team if you're a forward."

Gerstein was lined up at forward himself.

Jacob smiled. "But I guess you're the *star* of your team?" he said.

"Of course I am," Gerstein said. He adjusted his purple shorts and smoothed out his white shirt, pretending to spruce up to look his best.

Nate hoped they could shut this team down—especially Gerstein. Coach Toscano had worked on team defense before the game. He showed them how to cover each other and never get caught out of position.

Nate hoped everyone would remember once the game started.

The Racers had won the coin toss, and they came hard on the attack right from the opening kickoff.

It didn't take long to see that they were good athletes but not a very good team. They charged hard, but all of them wanted to dribble the ball and show off their fancy moves.

They kept losing the ball in the middle, with Clayton and Lian outfoxing them. Nate was amazed to see how quickly Lian was improving. He was a natural at soccer with his quick reactions.

But the Racers played *hard* defense. They crashed against players on tackles. Nate thought the referee should have called a couple of fouls right away. But it was about five or six minutes into the first half before he finally called one.

Clayton took the direct free kick from just inside Racers' territory. He looped a long kick toward the goal area. Heidi got to the ball and tried to control it, but a big Racers' fullback was right with her and managed to knock the ball away.

Jacob darted free from his defender and took control of the ball. He couldn't see anyone open, and so he took a rather long shot. The ball glanced off the legs of one of the Racers' fullbacks and the goalie chased after it.

But Henry was coming hard from the side. He and the goalie arrived at the same time, and they fought for control of the ball. The goalie tried to dive for it, but Henry managed to flick it away.

For a moment the ball was rolling free across the goal area. Heidi was racing toward it with a defender right on her. She slid across the grass and stabbed at the ball with her right foot.

She hit it pretty well and drove it toward the goal.

The goalie was right there in good position. He reached down and should have had the ball. But he didn't get in front of it, and it glanced off his arm. He had slowed it, but it still had enough speed left to roll into the goal.

*"Way to go!"* Jacob yelled, and Nate ran halfway up the field to tell Heidi what a great play she had made.

She yelled to him, "That's okay, Nate. You don't have to hug me. In fact, I'd rather you didn't." She and Nate both laughed.

This felt good.

After the drubbing the team had taken the day before, it was nice to get ahead today.

And things soon got better. Clayton made a great move and dribbled past his defender. He passed off to Heidi, took a return pass, and broke toward the goal. When the goalie charged out to meet him, Clayton made a perfect chip shot, looping the ball just over the goalie's head and into the net.

*2 to 0!*

And Nate liked to see that his fullbacks were dropping back quickly and playing hard-nosed defense. Nate kept shouting to them, helping them see what they had to do.

But he also yelled to them when they did things right.

The feeling on the team was good. And

Nate thought he was learning how to lead the defense. Heidi may have been joking about the positive stuff, but she was right. He could see that the players liked being told what they had done right.

By halftime the score was 3 to 0.

Clayton scored his second goal of the day, and he looked happy. He was really getting the hang of playing midfield. He could actually do more from that position, because it gave him more freedom to play a bigger part of the field.

As the players walked off the field, he told Nate, "The coach was right. I can do more from midfield than I did at forward. I still get my shots."

That was good news. When the coach had switched Clayton from forward to midfield Clayton had been very upset. But things were looking up.

The coach had also let Billy start the game for a change, and Billy had done a good job on defense. He was feeling extra cocky.

"I know how to make the Racers into a

better team," Billy was telling everyone. "Someone ought to wad up a pair of those ugly purple shorts and stuff them in Gerstein's mouth."

Everyone laughed, and then Jared said in his calm voice, "Nothing's going to help those guys. They stink. They don't belong on the same field with us."

But Nate worried just a little about that. He knew the Racers didn't play team soccer, but they had some very good players.

"Let's not start counting the victory yet," he told Billy and Jared. "We've gotta keep playing tough defense."

Brian had pulled off his goggles and was wiping the sweat from the lenses. "Nate thinks he's our coach," he said.

"No, I don't. But we can't let up. One year in the European Championships Spain had a three-goal lead over—"

"Okay, okay. Don't tell us another one of your soccer stories," Jared said. "We don't *read* about soccer; we play it."

Nate shut his mouth.

He just wished the game meant as much to the rest of the players as it did to him. There was nothing wrong with learning all he could about the game—by playing *and* from books.

And in the second half he found he hadn't been wrong.

Now that the team had its good lead, everyone wanted to get in on the attack. Once again, the fullbacks were moving too far up the field. No one wanted to stay back on defense.

And it finally backfired on them.

A Racers' fullback made a steal and quickly cleared the ball with a long kick. Gerstein saw what was coming and broke down the field. He got behind the Angel Park defenders and charged all out toward the goal.

Nate rushed toward him, and Gerstein got a little rattled. He tried to shoot when he was still moving too fast, and he didn't really hit the ball cleanly. It sliced away from him and went wide of the goal.

But the Pride had gotten lucky, and Nate let his fullbacks know it.

"Brian, you can't let *anybody* get behind you," he yelled. "You're the sweeper. What were you doing?"

"Okay, okay. I blew it," Brian said.

Nate backed off. But he didn't see the fullbacks change anything. They had nearly been burned, but they were soon getting themselves out of position again.

When the Racers stole a pass at midfield, Brian was slow to get back, and Cactus Hills drove the ball down the field with a long lead pass.

One of the forwards headed the ball back toward Gerstein, and he dribbled into the middle and got clear for a shot.

Brian tried to get back, but he was late, and Nate was left as the only player between Gerstein and the goal. Gerstein showed then that he *could* shoot the ball.

He dribbled forward a few steps and then *zapped* the ball, low and fast. This time he had caught it just right, and it shot past Nate before he could react.

Gerstein ran toward him and yelled, "Hey, goalie, you're not as *hot* as you think you are. We're not out of this game yet."

"You would be if I weren't the only one who plays defense around here," Nate yelled back at him.

But that didn't go over well.

Brian spun around and said, "What are you talking about, Nate? We're playing defense."

"Not much, you're not."

Nate didn't care. He had tried to be nice to these guys, but that didn't work. Someone had to tell them what they were doing wrong.

He looked over and saw the coach shaking his head. He had obviously seen the jawing going on.

Nate turned his back and kicked at the grass.

If the coach wanted him to *lead* without yelling at the players, he had better find some players who wouldn't keep making the same stupid mistakes!

# ★ 5 ★

# A Better Way

---

Nate decided he'd better shut his mouth before the coach took him out again—and the Pride blew another game.

But his patience was tested in the next few minutes.

Jimmy Gerstein announced, "Look out, *Pride,* I'm gonna get some more. We're going to win this game. What are you going to call yourselves then? The *Shame?*"

The Angel Park players were sick of the guy.

And then Nate saw Gerstein trip Tammy on purpose.

The Racers were on attack, but Gerstein was away from the ball. He broke behind Tammy, and when she tried to spin to catch up with him, he dragged his leg across her ankle and knocked her flat on the ground.

Tammy hit hard, but she bounced right up.

She was furious. She jumped up and looked around for a foul call, but the referee and the linesmen hadn't seen it. Just then Gerstein took a pass in front of the goal area, and Brian raced up to mark him.

Gerstein did get a shot off, but it glanced off Brian's leg and flew over the goal line, wide of the goal. That meant a corner kick for the Racers.

By now Tammy was pointing a finger in Gerstein's face. "You did that on purpose!" she said. Her face was red, and she was limping a little on the ankle he had hit.

"Who, me?" he said, and he gave her a big, fake smile.

Nate could see that she was ready to rip

into the guy, no matter how much smaller she was.

But she had to get ready for the kick, and she was on Gerstein like a blanket.

Gerstein tried to break loose and run to the corner of the goal, but Tammy went with him. As he leaped into the air to head the pass, she jumped too. She was still mad, and she jumped right into his back.

The whistle sounded, and Nate knew what was coming.

Penalty shot.

Gerstein laughed the whole time he was setting up. He knew he had gotten Tammy so angry that she had done something stupid. And that was just what he wanted.

Nate set up to stop the penalty shot. His only chance was to gamble by cutting off one side of the goal or the other and then to hope he guessed right. But Gerstein knew that game. He angled as though he were going for the right side of the goal, but then he brought his leg across and whipped the ball into the left side.

Nate took the fake and dove in the wrong direction. The ball slammed into the net behind him, and now the score was 3 to 2.

Nate got up slowly. He knew his chances hadn't been good to stop the penalty shot, but he just wished he had never had to try. Still, he didn't want Tammy to get down on herself.

"That's all right, Tammy," he yelled. "I saw what Gerstein did. But don't let him get to you again. We gotta be tough now. We've got about five minutes to go."

"That's more than enough time," Gerstein yelled to Nate. "We're coming hard, and you can't stop us."

Nate wondered if the guy wasn't right. But at least the Pride was willing to play defense now.

"Okay, Brian, Tammy," Nate shouted. "Let's be tough up the middle. Let's not give 'em any lanes at all."

"All right," Brian yelled back, and Tammy nodded. She had lost her cool before, but now she seemed to have her mind made up not to mess up again.

"Trenton, be careful," Nate shouted. "Stay right on their wing. Keep him on the touchline. And cut off the angle on their center passes. Same with you, Sterling. Let's not give them any room to breathe."

Sterling yelled to Clayton, "Help us out on defense. Once they get the ball, we've all got to get back very fast. You too, Lian."

Everyone was agreeing, yelling back and forth. Five minutes of tough defense would do it. They didn't have to score if they could keep the Racers away from their own goal.

But the Racers also knew that they had to take some chances and go strong on attack. They were soon coming hard.

When a Racers' wing made a touchline run, Chris Baca was right with him. And Sterling stayed wide to help out. They kept the wing outside, and when he tried to pass, Sterling made the steal and cleared the ball with a long kick upfield.

It was just what Nate had told him to do.

But the Racers came right back on attack.

Clayton met the midfielder, and he made things tough for him. The guy thought he was a good dribbler, but Clayton played it smart. He didn't close in tight where he might get beat, but he kept cutting off any chances the attacker had to pass the ball.

And then, suddenly, Clayton jumped in and made the tackle.

He knocked the ball away and leaped after it. But he didn't try anything fancy.

Clayton waited for Tanya Gardner and some of his other teammates to come up for help, and then he made a good, safe pass to Chris on the wing. Chris dropped the ball back to Clayton, and let him control it in the middle.

The Pride took the ball up the field slowly. Jacob came up and took a good pass. Instead of trying to push into the thick of things, he brought the ball back toward midfield. The defender was giving him room, so he took his time.

Then Jacob flipped the ball back to Clayton, who was the least likely player to lose the ball.

All this was taking time off the clock. And Nate liked seeing the ball at the other end of the field. He was starting to feel that the team was coming together, understanding what it took to win.

What he also noticed was that his fullbacks were staying back in a strong position, just in case the Racers got control of the ball.

And that's how the game kept going.

The Racers were getting frustrated. And maybe a little desperate.

They needed to take some good shots to have a chance, and the Pride kept clearing the ball all the way up the field and forcing the Racers to start over. Valuable seconds were ticking away.

When the Racers did get within shooting range, the defense was piled in tight. They struggled to get off shots with any zip on them, and when they did shoot, they had to get the ball past too many defenders to have much of a chance.

"That's it. That's it," Nate kept yelling. "Pick him up, Tanya. Okay, help me out, Billy. Cut off his angle. Double on him, Sterling."

And the team responded. What Nate was telling them was working, and they seemed to accept that. It was beautiful to see how the whole team was working as a unit.

The Racers were going all out. All their fullbacks were on attack, trying to make up for the stacked defense, and everyone was pouring toward the goal area.

And then, suddenly, the Racers' gamble backfired.

Sterling stepped in, stopped a pass, spun around, and then booted the ball upfield. Lian saw what was happening and was the first to break for the ball. He outran the big Racers' fullback who tried to stay with him.

Lian got to the ball and kicked it downfield, and then raced after it again.

Lian was too quick for the fullback, and

he got a good lead on the guy. As he picked up the ball, he slowed just a little to get under control, and then he dribbled hard and straight toward the goal.

The goalie broke toward him, and the fullback finally caught up. But without warning, Lian suddenly heeled the ball, dropping it straight back as though he knew exactly what was happening behind him.

And he was right.

Clayton had made the long run and was trailing the play. He picked up the ball on the run and broke right past the two defenders.

He slammed the ball into the open net!

Clayton spun around and pointed at Lian. *"Beautiful!"* he screamed. "Brilliant pass!"

All the Angel Park players were charging into the goal area now, jumping on each other, cheering for Clayton and Lian and going wild.

Nate stayed at his end of the field, but he waved his arms and shouted.

He felt great!

And the Racers knew they were beaten.

They didn't come back with the same fury, even though they tried to work hard. They didn't even come close to scoring. The game ended 4 to 2, and the Pride was still alive in the tournament.

When the players came off the field, Coach Toscano was beaming. He congratulated every player, one by one. And then he had them all sit down.

"Okay, team, we play for the consolation championship on Saturday. That gives us tomorrow to practice, and we do have some things we need to work on. But I'm very happy with what I saw today. Give yourselves a cheer."

All the players shouted.

"Lian," the coach said, "I didn't hear Clayton yell to you. How did you know he was behind you."

"I don't know. I heard someone running, and—I don't know—I just felt like it was him."

"I was just going to call out, Coach,"

Clayton said, "and then there was the ball—like he had eyes in the back of his head."

"Yes. Exactly. That's soccer. Somehow—on a really good team—the players know where everyone else is. They talk on the field. But they also have some feel for each other's moves. Maybe that's starting to happen to us."

Nate liked that.

Maybe the Pride was going to be all right.

Something was starting to happen.

# Time to Lead

===

*"However."*

The Angel Park players had all started talking to each other. Suddenly, the coach had their attention again.

"However—I'm still concerned about some things. We played solid defense in the first half. But then we let up. Against a better team, that letup could have cost us the game."

The coach looked around at everyone.

He waited while he let them think about that.

"Now," he said, "what are we going to do about it?"

No one answered.

The coach looked at Nate, who was sitting up front. "Nate, you're the team leader when it comes to defense. What are you going to do?"

"Well, we need to think about defense all the time—not just when we have the lead. It seems like we get thinking about scoring, and then, when we have to switch back to defense, we don't react fast enough."

"Yes. But what are you going to *do* about it?"

Nate was sort of ready for that question now. For two days he had been trying to think what he had to do, how he could lead, and he hadn't found the answer. But in the last few minutes of the game, he had begun to get an idea.

Now it was time to make it happen. The coach expected him to show his leadership *right now.*

"Coach," Nate said, "our next game is going to be a shutout."

Then he waited so everyone would have time to think about what he had said.

"I don't know what team we play on Saturday, but whoever it is, we're not going to give them a single goal. I know we can do it."

The coach chuckled a little. "Big talk doesn't win matches," he said.

"It's not just talk. We have great fullbacks, and when we get our whole team playing together—the way we did at the end of the game today—we're like a *wall*."

"You really think your fullbacks are that good?"

"Yes, I do."

"That's *right!*" Sterling shouted, and his fist shot in the air.

*"Right!"* Tammy yelled.

*"We'll do it!"* Brian said, and he jumped up.

And suddenly all the fullbacks—and Nate—were standing. They pumped their fists in the air and promised, "We'll shut 'em out!"

But Nate saw Adam Snarr and Chris look at each other and smile, as if to say, "Oh, sure."

"What's the matter?" Nate asked them. "Don't you think we can do it?"

They weren't about to answer, but they were still smiling.

"We'll do it!" Sterling vowed again, and all the fullbacks agreed.

But the coach said, "Fullbacks are the key to defense, but they can't shut a team out by themselves. *Everybody* has to be involved."

"That's right," Nate said. "If you'll all play the way you did at the end of the game today—and if you'll listen when I tell you where to cover—we can do it!"

Nate could see that the team was starting to believe. Everyone knew what a tough time the Racers had had once the Pride really concentrated on defense.

"Okay, now wait a minute," the coach said. The kids were sitting in a half circle, and he was in the middle. "Cheering is great, but you have to make it happen. You have to listen to Nate. And you can't get beat getting back, not even once."

The players were all nodding. Nate had

the feeling they really were making up their minds to do it.

"We need to get the pressure on attack," Coach Toscano said, "but we can never let down on that switch into defense. That's what we'll work on in practice tomorrow."

Nate liked that.

He knew that he needed the coach's support if he was going to lead the team. But he also knew he had done something right— something positive. The team had something to work for now, and they were excited about it.

"I want to talk to all the fullbacks for just a couple of minutes before you go," Nate said.

And so the fullbacks stayed.

"We've got to be more clear about a few things," Nate said.

He had everyone sit down, and they talked about their strategies on corner kicks and how to keep coverage when a team got a throw-in or a goal kick. And they talked about signals they could use to let each other know what they were going to do.

For once, Nate wasn't doing all the talking. He knew more than they did, but he listened to everyone's ideas.

He really felt like a leader.

And when he went home that afternoon, he was still excited.

No one was home when he first got there, but his dad came in not long after.

"Hey, Dad, we won today," Nate told him. "Four to two."

"That's good, son," Mr. Matheson said. "Is your mom home yet?" He was loosening his tie. Nate thought he looked tired.

"No."

"Her plane must have been late. She thought she'd be in by now. I think there are some frozen dinners in the freezer. Should we heat up a couple of those?"

"Sure."

Dad walked on into the kitchen.

Nate followed him. "The coach says I have to be the leader on defense. That's what I'm trying to do."

"Are you still playing goalie most of the time?"

"*All* the time, Dad. That's what I am."

His dad was digging around in the freezer. "Turkey or beef?" he said.

"I don't care."

Dad pulled out one of the packages and started reading the instructions.

"The coach told me that I could be *really* good if I keep working hard every year—all the way through the higher leagues. And then, what I've been thinking is that I could play college soccer at a school that has a good team. Maybe I could even go to England or—"

Mr. Matheson suddenly looked up from the package he was reading. He looked surprised. "Nate, you can't pick your college by the *soccer team*. You need to think about your education first." But then he laughed. "You have a few years to worry about that anyway."

"I know. But if I want to be a professional soccer player, I'll have to get all the experience I can. And I need to play for a really strong—"

"Nate, come on, be realistic. A kid from

this country isn't going to make a living that way. The Europeans and South Americans are a million miles ahead of us in soccer. You just can't compete with them. You'll see that when you get a little older."

"Dad, I already know that. But Americans are getting better. And it's what I want to do. It's the *only* thing I want to do."

"Okay, son, if you say so." But he was looking at the package again, and Nate knew that he didn't really take the idea seriously.

"Just don't think so much about soccer that you let your grades go," he added. "When you get a few years older, you'll see that that's the most important thing. Every kid thinks he's going to be a pro athlete someday. With me, it was baseball. And I had the same idea. I'm just glad I didn't let down in school, because I wouldn't have had any chance at all in baseball."

Nate knew that school was important. He had always gotten good grades. But why couldn't his dad understand how much soccer meant to him? Sure, lots of kids *talked* about being professional ballplayers, but not all of them worked the way Nate did—or had the talent.

"Dad, we're playing for the consolation championship on Saturday. Can you come?"

"What time?"

"I'm not sure yet. I'll find out tomorrow."

"Well, I don't know. I'm so far behind at the office I may need to go in and try to catch up. If it's late in the day, I might be able to get over. But if it's in the morning, I wouldn't count on me. Maybe your mom can go over."

"She won't."

"What?" Dad had begun to tear part of the tin foil back on the frozen meal package, but now he looked at Nate.

"She won't come, Dad. She doesn't care. And you don't either."

"Oh, come on, son. Don't start that again. Both of us put in long hours at our jobs. We can't help that."

"You could come to my games if you wanted to. Most of the parents do."

"We *do* come when we can, Nate. I thought we talked this all out before."

Yeah, Nate told himself. We talked it out. And you said the same thing: "I'll come when I can."

And that turned out to be almost never.

But Nate didn't say what he was thinking.

"You know, Nate, your mom and I put away money every month for your college fund. If you get into a first-rate college, the money is going to be there. And you'll be set for life. Maybe some of those parents who hang out at your soccer games aren't looking that far ahead. Maybe they aren't thinking about their kid's future as much as we are."

"I just don't see why you have to work so many hours all the time."

"To provide for you, for one thing." And now Dad was mad. "I don't notice that you *lack* for anything. How many of your friends live in houses like this?"

"I don't care about this house, Dad! That's the last thing I care about. But then, you don't know what I *do* care about. I try to tell you, but you won't listen."

"*Soccer!* That's the only thing you ever talk about. And it's just plain stupid, Nate. There are a whole lot of things in this world more important than soccer. You've got to get that straight someday."

"You're the one who doesn't know what's important!"

Nate walked from the room.

But he felt sick already. He had let his mouth go again. And that would only make things worse with his dad.

Why couldn't he just learn to shut up sometimes?

## ★ 7 ★

# Time to Play

Nate didn't want to be mad at his dad. And he didn't want his dad to be mad at him.

He wished he hadn't said anything.

So Nate avoided the whole topic the rest of the evening. And his dad didn't say much to him. He had brought work home that night, and he went to the office very early the next morning.

After school that next day, Nate practiced with the team.

The coach worked with the players on "team defense." He showed them ways to help each other out. They could slip away from an attacker and double the player with the ball—as long as others helped cover.

The coach also showed the players how to move into a zone defense instead of a man-to-man one once the attack got close to the goal area. They each had to mark someone, but they could release their assigned players to the next zone and keep up a tight, closed line.

Nate's job was to watch all this and shout out switches, or quickly correct mistakes when an attacker was left uncovered.

The best thing was, it worked!

The players got very excited when they saw how they could shut down an attack— and they liked the way it felt to work so closely together. Everyone felt great when practice was over, and they were confident they really could get that shutout. Or at least most of them were.

"Nate," Heidi said, "do you really think we can beat Paseo? They won this tournament last year."

"Maybe they're not as good this year," Jacob said.

"Yeah, maybe," Nate said, "but they lost the first game in overtime, and their best player—Oshima—couldn't play. He's going to play tomorrow."

"I know Oshima," Jacob said. "He played second base for their baseball team. He's a good ballplayer."

"Well, he's a *great* soccer player," Heidi said.

"Yeah, he is," Nate said. "But we can still win. Or at least we can if you forwards can get a goal. The defense is going to shut them out."

"Do you *really* think we can do that?" Jacob asked.

"Yeah, I do. Don't you?"

"I don't know. Everyone we've played has scored on us. I just don't know if we can keep up our concentration that long and never make a mistake."

"Well, you'll find out tomorrow. We're going to do it," Nate said, and he meant it.

By game time the next day, however, he was really nervous. He had talked big, and now he knew he had to prove that he could do more than talk. And the team had to believe with him—every single player.

And then there was that other fear. What if the fullbacks—the whole team—played tough, and *he* messed up? He really felt he had to play the game of his life.

Besides, Nate had the feeling the whole season might depend on this game.

It wasn't a league game, but it was a chance for the Pride to pick up a lot of confidence. And that's what they needed as they were about to start a new season.

The game was starting at noon. Mr. Matheson had left early for his office that morning. And Mom said she had a very busy day ahead.

Neither one said they *wouldn't* come. But Nate knew. It was the same old thing.

When the game started, Nate was nervous. He found himself pacing back and forth while his team was on attack. And then, when the Paseo Bandits came toward him, he was on his toes, ready, but his stomach was in knots.

What he saw he liked, however.

The fullbacks were keeping their positions, dropping quickly into defense. And the midfielders and forwards were really making the Bandits work to get the ball up the field.

Once Paseo got the ball near the Angel Park goal, the defense was making a good transition into a match-up zone, covering people and trading them off through the zones.

And it worked.

Paseo was knocking its head against a wall. It didn't get off a good shot during the first fifteen minutes of the game.

But then, neither did the Pride.

The battle was all defense, and both teams struggled to get the ball deep. Clayton and Oshima were marking each other in the middle of the field, and they were putting on a *show*. Both had amazing moves, and both were good defenders.

But they were stopping each other, and neither one was getting a chance to shoot.

Finally the Bandits had a throw-in, and Oshima put a good fake on Clayton and got free for the ball. Oshima crossed the field and went to the touchline, passed off to his wing, and then broke upfield for a lead pass.

Clayton was right with him, but he stumbled for a moment and Oshima made a good run deep into Pride territory. Sterling picked him up and forced him wide of the goal area, but Oshima was a master of cuts.

Just when he seemed beyond the chance for a shot, he made a reverse cut and then slammed the ball with his left foot. It seemed only a center pass at first, but he had put a hook on the ball, and it curved toward the goal.

Nate darted to the corner of the goal and leaped. He had no chance to catch the ball, but he jumped as high as he could, reached up, slammed it with his fist, and sent it high over the goal.

It was a close call, and Nate had made a great save. But now came the corner kick. Oshima was as good a header as there was in the league. And he was moving into position, looking for his chance.

The left wing, a tiny girl but a great kicker, lofted a center pass from the corner. Jared was right on Oshima, and Brian got up in the air with him too.

But it was the other forward, a slower boy, who was closest to the pass. He saw that he couldn't head the ball in, so he controlled it off his chest and then tried to get free for a shot.

Tammy was all over him, and Brian left Oshima and closed quickly. But the forward didn't shoot. He pushed the ball with the outside of his foot and led Oshima, who broke away from Jared. Oshima didn't have much room, but he took advantage of the little lead he had gotten on Jared. He blasted a shot on the goal.

*Slam!*

Oshima was not ten feet from Nate, and he hit the ball hard. But Nate reacted instantly.

His hand flashed out just in time and

caught the ball square. It bounced in front of Nate, and he chased it down quickly. He grabbed it and ran forward and then punted it well down the field.

"Great save!" his teammates yelled to him as they headed up the field. And the shutout was still alive.

It was the closest the Bandits got to a score during the first half. They kept coming and coming, but the defense held up time and time again. They were working like a machine together, and they all felt that they could get their shutout.

The only problem was that they had not even come close to scoring. The defense was solid, but nothing was really happening on attack.

At halftime the coach talked to the players about that. "Okay, we're playing *great* defense. That's the heart of good soccer. But you can't win unless you score. You have to switch into attack the instant you get control of the ball."

"Coach, we can't let up on our defense," Nate said. He knew what could happen if everyone started thinking attack and forgetting what they had been doing in the first half.

"No, we can't. But you can't get the ball and then take a deep breath and say, 'At least they didn't score.' You have to switch gears immediately and see what's open upfield."

"They're doing what we're doing on defense," Sterling said. "They get back quick, and they set up."

"If we let them beat us back every time, we can't get the edge on them," Coach Toscano said. "Right at the moment we take control of the ball things have to happen. We all have to run, get upfield, run to space, get open, look for a chance."

Nate knew that was right. And he knew the team had to get a goal somehow. But he feared that the team would go back to its old ways if they didn't keep concentrating on defense.

Suddenly Nate's attention was taken away from the coach.

He had just spotted his father walking

across the park toward the soccer field. There were bleachers on each side of the field, and his dad slipped into the seats on the Bandits' side.

He sat by himself at the end of the bleachers. It was a rather cool day, and most of the fans were wearing jackets and jeans. But there was his dad in a dark suit and a fancy, flowered tie. He didn't exactly look like a soccer fan, but he was *there*.

Heidi nudged Nate. "Isn't that your dad?" she asked.

Nate nodded. He had gotten into the flow of things during the game, and he had gradually relaxed, but now he was suddenly more nervous than ever.

"We've gotta win," he said to Heidi. "It's important."

"Why, Nate?" Jacob asked.

"We just have to. You guys have got to get a goal somehow."

"I don't think we can get a whole goal," Heidi said, and she sounded serious.

"What do you mean?" Nate asked.

"A whole goal is hard. But maybe Jacob could get half of one, and I could get another half, and together, that would give us one."

Nate shook his head. He should have learned by now that something strange could come out of Heidi's mouth at any time. But she always seemed to catch him by surprise.

"You have a weird mind," Jacob said. He started to laugh.

But Heidi still held a straight face. "Hey, it's a *whole* new approach to the game," she said. "We could become the greatest half-goal shooters in the world. Just think of it! And maybe go from there to four players each getting one-fourth goals, or eight . . . nah, that's going too far."

Nate smiled a little. But he was too nervous to laugh at her. He really wanted this game to come out right. He *couldn't* mess up now.

His dad was there.

# Time to Win

The second half started out with the two defenses still in control. But gradually the attacking teams started taking more chances.

Neither defense was quite as packed in, and neither team was getting back as quickly as they had earlier in the match.

Both attacks were getting more pressure on the other goal, but neither team could come up with a score.

And then Jacob stole a pass just as the Bandits had moved onto attack. Some of the Paseo players had broken upfield quickly when their team got the ball, and the Pride was suddenly in a strong position.

The Paseo sweeper marked Jacob as soon as he stole the ball, but Heidi was open for a shot, and Jacob hit her immediately.

Heidi fired, and the shot looked good, but it hit the right goalpost and rebounded off to the right.

The ball bounced directly to a Bandit fullback, and he cleared the ball quickly up the field.

Suddenly everything was reversed. The players had all been switching back to head the other way when everything turned again.

The Bandits got the advantage this time. The left wing got up the field and passed the ball into the center, where Oshima was running hard.

Sterling was with him and could match his speed, but Oshima saw that and slowed.

He let the Pride defense think he was going to wait for his teammates to catch him, and then, suddenly, he broke forward again, all out.

He got by Sterling, but Tammy and Brian

had gotten back now, and they picked him up.

Still, everything was confused for the moment, with no one in position for a strong defense. And with Oshima doubled, Nate knew someone had to be open. He didn't like the look of what was developing.

Oshima angled toward the touchline. Brian stayed on him and kept him from darting straight for the goal.

But a wing was coming up to the right of him, and Oshima passed off. Then, without the ball, Oshima dashed toward the goal.

The wing saw Oshima break, and he kicked a high center pass.

For Nate it was a moment of decision.

He could stay back and . . .

But then he knew his only chance was to get to the ball before Oshima did. He charged forward and leaped high in the air. He lifted his knee to protect himself, the way the coach had taught him to do.

At the same moment Oshima jumped and tried to get up high enough to head the ball.

But Nate was flying. He reached over the top of Oshima's head and plucked the ball out of the air.

Nate came down with the ball wrapped up, and he remembered what the coach had said. "Think attack—*instantly.*"

He tossed the ball out to Billy, who was in the game at fullback.

Billy took the pass and turned upfield, but he was not quite quick enough. The Bandit wing was on top of him. He dove across the grass and slammed the ball away from Billy with a good slide tackle.

A Bandit forward controlled the ball, cut it behind him, and broke to the left. He got himself free for just a second and blasted a hard left-footed shot.

Nate dove, stretched all the way out, and caught the ball with the tips of his fingers. But as he came down, the ball jarred loose in front of the goal. It was rolling free, and Nate was still on the ground.

Oshima had charged the goal for a follow-up, and he was about to bang the ball home when Nate reacted. He scrambled up and got a foot under him, and then dove at the ball as it rolled away from him.

He got his hands on the ball just as Oshima kicked, and he took a hard blow to his forearm.

But he had the ball.

His arm was screaming with pain. Still, he jumped up, ran a couple of steps, and then punted the ball to midfield.

Then he dropped to the grass and grabbed his arm.

"Are you all right?" Brian yelled.

There was no time to talk, though. The Bandits had taken control and were coming back, driving hard. Nate got up. He got ready. "I'm okay. Cover the forward. Number twenty."

This time the Pride defense got back and in position. But the wing centered a pass in front of the goal, and Oshima went up to head it.

Tammy went up with him, but she was shorter. Oshima blasted the ball at the goal.

Nate was in the air again—stretched to his left. And one more time, he slammed the ball away.

This time Henry got to it, and the Pride went on attack.

Nate watched to make sure the ball was safely upfield. Then he checked his arm. The skin was broken a little, but he knew it was not serious. The pain was going away already.

But Nate was exhausted. He took some deep breaths, and he wondered how soon the attack would come again.

And then something happened he hadn't expected—had never even thought was possible.

His dad had left the bleachers and had come down to Nate's end of the field. He was clapping his hands and yelling. "Nate! Nate!" he shouted. "That was incredible. Fantastic. You're *great!*"

Nate realized that he had never played better—never made four better saves when the game was on the line. But he hadn't really thought about it at the time. He hadn't *had* time.

But there was his dad still yelling. "Keep it up, son. You can beat these guys!"

Tears came to Nate's eyes. He couldn't help it. He had never seen his father this excited . . . about *anything*.

But he couldn't think about all that right now. He had to be ready.

And his team needed to score.

*Somehow* they just had to score.

Clayton knew that too. And he was the leader of the attack. Nate could see that Clayton's style of play had begun to change. It was as though he had said to himself, "If Nate can keep our shutout alive, I can do what it takes to get us a goal."

The ball was near the center line when Clayton guessed right on a Bandits' pass and ran to it before the attacker could.

He broke straight up the field with the ball, but two defenders were waiting to pick him up.

Henry came down the right wing and yelled, "Clayton. Here."

Clayton stroked with his leg, as though he were going to kick the ball to Henry. But he faked and swung over the ball. And then—*bang*—he broke between the two defenders and shot into the clear.

The Bandit sweeper had picked up Henry, but now he broke toward the goal to cover Clayton.

Clayton saw that and passed off to Henry, who dribbled hard toward the goal until the sweeper committed back the other way.

And then *zap*, he hit Clayton in the clear.

Clayton didn't lose his cool. He saw the goalie dart toward the left corner, the widest side. He paused just a fraction of a second and then drove the ball behind the goalie.

*Score!*

Nate ran all the way up the field to be

with the rest of his team. They went out of their minds, piling on top of each other.

But Nate was already yelling, *"Defense, everyone. Defense!"*

And the team played excellent defense. They stacked into their zones, and they listened as Nate yelled out to them.

"Tanya, pick up the wing. Drop back. Switch now, Trenton. Switch."

It was a beautiful thing to see. The defense was a solid wall, but also a moving, reacting, powerful force, and Nate was making it all happen.

As the Bandits tried everything they could, the seconds ticked away.

And then the whistle was blowing and the Pride had won!

Everyone jumped all over each other.

Except Nate.

His dad had run onto the field. Nate saw him and ran straight for him.

They stopped in front of each other for a moment, and Nate didn't know what he should do. But then his dad had him in his arms. "I didn't know, Nate," he said. "I just didn't know you were this good. *No wonder* you love this game."

Nate didn't say anything. He couldn't.

But that afternoon he and his dad talked. School still had to be number one, but maybe Nate could attend some summer soccer camps, and why shouldn't he choose a college someday that had a great team? Maybe he would never be a professional, but he had a chance to be a great player, and it was worth the effort.

Later on, Heidi and Jacob came over.

Mostly, the three of them talked about the season.

"You know what?" Jacob told Nate and Heidi. "Soccer is going to turn out to be all right. It could be as fun as baseball was."

But Nate thought he was nuts. *"Baseball? You gotta be kidding. You don't get action like we had today in a baseball game!"*

"Yeah, that's true. But baseball gets tense. You've got all that time to think. And you stand up there and wait for a pitch, and your heart is beating so loud you can hardly stand it."

"Maybe we could think up a new game," Heidi said. "Maybe we could run around a soccer field with bats in our hands, and other guys pitching, and umpires everywhere, and . . . nah, I guess it wouldn't work."

"You're weird, Heidi," Jacob said. "Really weird."

But they all laughed.

And then Jacob said, "Well, baseball is a great game. But I gotta admit, I really like soccer."

Nate and Heidi grinned.

"And you know," Jacob added, "we could be good this year. *Really* good!"

"Not just *could be*," Nate said. "We're *going to be* good."

And he was sure of it.

# Angel Park Soccer Strategies

Soccer, like football and basketball, is a game of game plans, of strategies. Both professionals and amateurs use strategies to give themselves a general sense of what to do *as a team*. Without teamwork and strategy, soccer games would only be a bunch of people running around a field, kicking a ball back and forth.

This is why players have particular jobs to do, either scoring goals or defending against goals. This makes the game more interesting—and more challenging. When a player is running upfield with the ball, he will almost always be cut off before he scores a goal himself. This is why players learn strategies. When the time comes, they'll know what to do. They'll know where their teammates are without even looking.

Or at least that's the idea. The success of the strategies depends on the skill of the players. The strategies we've presented here, in these diagrams, are standard game plans that the Angel Park Pride might attempt to use in a game. If you think your team could profit from a little strategic thinking, show these to your coach. Give them a try. Good luck!

# Kickoff

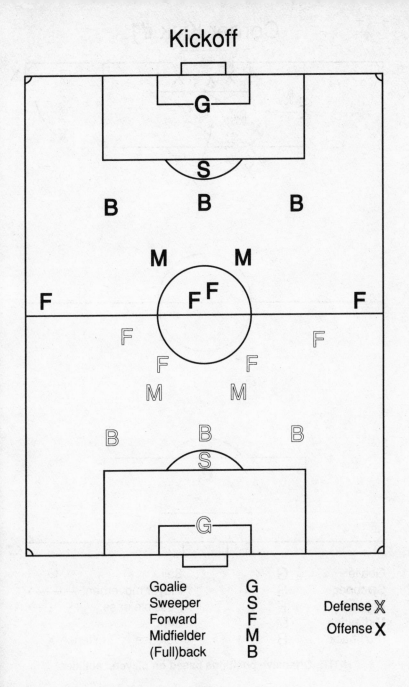

| | |
|---|---|
| Goalie | G |
| Sweeper | S |
| Forward | F |
| Midfielder | M |
| (Full)back | B |

Defense X

Offense X

# Corner Kick #1

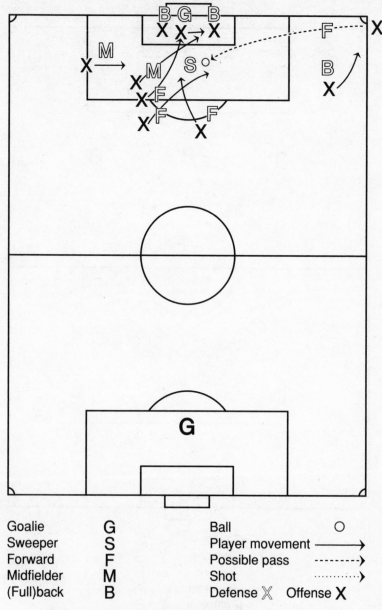

| | | |
|---|---|---|
| Goalie | **G** | Ball ○ |
| Sweeper | **S** | Player movement ⟶ |
| Forward | **F** | Possible pass ╌╌╌> |
| Midfielder | **M** | Shot ·······> |
| (Full)back | **B** | Defense ✕  Offense **X** |

<u>**NOTE:**</u> **Offensive positions based on players' abilities**

# Corner Kick #2

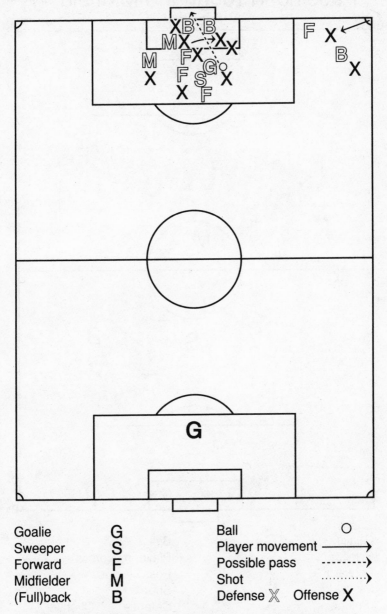

| Goalie | G | Ball | ○ |
| Sweeper | S | Player movement | ⟶ |
| Forward | F | Possible pass | ⤏ |
| Midfielder | M | Shot | ⋯⟩ |
| (Full)back | B | Defense ✕ Offense **X** |

**NOTE:** Offensive positions based on players' abilities

99

# Passing Through the Midfield #1

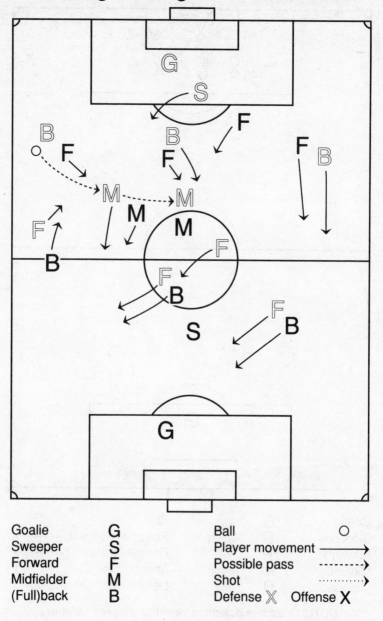

| | | | |
|---|---|---|---|
| Goalie | G | Ball | O |
| Sweeper | S | Player movement | ———→ |
| Forward | F | Possible pass | ------→ |
| Midfielder | M | Shot | ·······→ |
| (Full)back | B | Defense X Offense X | |

# Passing Through the Midfield #2

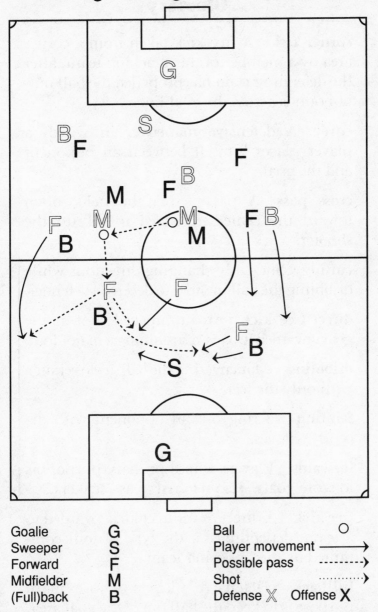

Goalie — G
Sweeper — S
Forward — F
Midfielder — M
(Full)back — B

Ball — O
Player movement — →
Possible pass — ------→
Shot — ........→
Defense X  Offense X

# Glossary

**corner kick**   A free kick taken from a corner area by a member of the attacking team, after the defending team has propelled the ball out-of-bounds across the goal line.

**cover**   A defensive maneuver in which a player places himself between an opponent and the goal.

**cross pass**   A pass across the field, often toward the center, intended to set up the shooter.

**cutting**   Suddenly changing directions while dribbling the ball in order to deceive a defender.

**direct free kick**   An unimpeded shot at the goal, awarded to a team sustaining a major foul.

**dribbling**   Maneuvering the ball at close range with only the feet.

**feinting**   Faking out an opponent with deceptive moves.

**forwards**   Players whose primary purpose is to score goals. Also referred to as "strikers."

**free kick**   A direct *or* indirect kick awarded to a team, depending on the type of foul committed by the opposing team.

**fullbacks**   Defensive players whose main purpose is to keep the ball out of the goal area.

**goalkeeper**  The ultimate defender against attacks on the goal, and the only player allowed to use his hands.

**halfbacks**  See Midfielders.

**heading**  Propelling the ball with the head, especially the forehead.

**indirect free kick**  A shot at the goal involving at least two players, awarded to a team sustaining a minor foul.

**juggling**  A drill using the thighs, feet, ankles, or head to keep the ball in the air continuously.

**kickoff**  A center place kick which starts the action at the beginning of both the first and second halves or after a goal has been scored.

**marking**  Guarding a particular opponent.

**midfielders**  Players whose main purpose is to get the ball from the defensive players to the forwards. Also called "halfbacks."

**penalty kick**  A direct free kick awarded to a member of the attacking team from a spot 12 yards in front of the goal. All other players must stay outside the penalty area except for the goalie, who must remain stationary until the ball is in play.

**punt**   A drop kick made by the goalkeeper.

**shooting**   Making an attempt to score a goal.

**strikers**   See Forwards.

**sweeper**   The last player, besides the goal-keeper, to defend the goal against attack.

**tackling**   Stealing the ball from an opponent by using the feet or a shoulder charge.

**total soccer**   A system by which players are constantly shifting positions as the team shifts from offense to defense. Also called "position-less soccer."

**volley kick**   A kick made while the ball is still in the air.

**wall**   A defensive barrier of players who stand in front of the goal area to aid the goalkeeper against free kicks.

**wall pass**   This play involves a short pass from one teammate to another, followed by a return pass to the first player as he runs past the defender. Also called the "give-and-go."

**wingbacks**   Outside fullbacks.

**wingers**   Outside forwards.

DEAN HUGHES has written many books for children, including the popular *Nutty* stories and *Jelly's Circus*. He has also published such works of literary fiction for young adults as the highly acclaimed *Family Pose*. Writing keeps Mr. Hughes very busy, but he does find time to run and play golf—and he loves to watch almost all sports. His home is in Utah. He and his wife have three children, all in college.

*Play ball with the kids from Angel Park!*

# ANGEL PARK ALL-STARS™

## by Dean Hughes

Meet Kenny, Harlan, and Jacob—three talented young players on Angel Park's Little League team. They're in for plenty of fastball action…as well as fun and friendship. Collect them all! Watch for new titles and new sports coming soon!

✄ - - - - - - - - - - - - - - - - - - - - - - - - - - - - - - ✄

### *Available wherever books are sold, or use this coupon.*

| | | | | |
|---|---|---|---|---|
| _____ | 679-80426-9 | #1 | **Making the Team** | $2.95 |
| _____ | 679-80427-7 | #2 | **Big Base Hit** | $2.95 |
| _____ | 679-80428-5 | #3 | **Winning Streak** | $2.95 |
| _____ | 679-80429-3 | #4 | **What a Catch!** | $2.95 |
| _____ | 679-80430-7 | #5 | **Rookie Star** | $2.95 |
| _____ | 679-80431-5 | #6 | **Pressure Play** | $2.95 |
| _____ | 679-80432-3 | #7 | **Line Drive** | $2.95 |
| _____ | 679-80433-1 | #8 | **Championship Game** | $2.95 |
| _____ | 679-81536-8 | #9 | **Superstar Team** | $2.95 |
| _____ | 679-81537-6 | #10 | **Stroke of Luck** | $2.95 |
| _____ | 679-81538-4 | #11 | **Safe at First** | $2.95 |
| _____ | 679-81539-2 | #12 | **Up to Bat** | $2.95 |
| _____ | 679-81540-6 | #13 | **Play-off** | $2.95 |
| _____ | 679-81541-4 | #14 | **All Together Now** | $2.95 |

Alfred A. Knopf, Inc., P.O. Box 100, Westminster, MD 21157
Please send me the books I have checked above. I am enclosing
$_____ .
(Please add $2.00 for shipping and handling for the first book and 50¢ for each additional book.) Send check or money order—no cash or C.O.D.'s please. Prices are subject to change without notice. Valid in U.S. only. All orders are subject to availability of books.

Name _____

Address _____

City _____ State _____ Zip _____

Please allow at least 4 weeks for delivery.                    APAS 1